ISBN 979-8-9897701-7-5

Published by Hidden Hand Press
www.hiddenhandbooks.com

HIDDEN HAND PRESS

Teeth!

by Sebastian Gray

Part I:

An Uncommon Childhood

She comes to us in sleep. This was, at the first inception of that dark obsession which was to be my undoing, all I knew of her. If I had known, then, that it was not an angel I was calling to me all those dark, delirious nights of my childhood, not divinity or transcendence, or even the mundane reward of a copper coin, but the spectre of my own ruination, then perhaps I could have averted this fate. I may have dammed the river Styx and washed up on some purgatorial bank, some ways downstream of Hell. Or else I was born cursed, and destined for naught but this bloody end since I first began to shed my milk teeth, at which point my troubles began.

I was cared for, in my early days, by a base and mindless hireling called Constance, a solid golem of female flesh who stank of sour dough and delighted in telling me stories of dreadful things. I know not if these tales were intended to haunt my childhood, or were a misguided attempt at inspiring such a sense of whimsy or enchantment as is often cultivated, for some purpose, in the children of the lower classes. Surely I found no whimsy in Constance's stories. And of the other, the only enchantment under which I have fallen in my life has been of a decidedly more sinister nature.

These tales of Constance's which so unshaped with terror my primordial mind were chiefly concerned with a dreadful creature of female aspect who, I was able to interpret from my nurse's circuitous ramblings, was primarily engaged with the capture and amassment of human teeth. She came in the dark of night, slipping into the beds of sleeping children, to purchase at some paltry price those cracked remnants of their bicuspids and molars, canines and premolars. My sleep, which had always been fitful, was further burdened by apparitions of seraphic monstrosities seeking to harvest my infant teeth for some outrageous purpose I could not aspire to comprehend. These night terrors could only be alleviated by a brand of soothing syrup my mother purchased at the local apothecary, the same solution which had once assuaged the exquisite agony of teething.

I did wonder, even then, at the question which was to burden me for years into my adulthood. Did my terror originate with Constance's stories, or did they merely give shape and context to some unknown horror which had long haunted my subconscious?

My sainted mother threatened Constance with dismissal should she continue to burden my youthful psyche with these horrific amusements. Yet the great cloddish woman persisted, supplying me with tales of terror, feeding my obsession as if with poison funnelled nightly into my ear. Though as bovine in intellect as in aspect, Constance nonetheless inspired some sentiment of obligation in my mother since her late father had once been of service to our family, and so my mother persisted in employing her despite the woman's crass superstitions.

My mother was a delicate woman who depended greatly on her servants. The loss of my father in an unlikely fall from a high window had left her in a fragile state. Less than three years later her nerve was broken completely when my sister

Antigone was fatally poisoned, having drunk down an entire bottle of my mother's favourite Parisian perfume. From then on she rarely left the house or engaged with society, and my childhood was a largely melancholy one. I had little to fill my days, then, but to dwell on various terrors of which the Tooth Fairy was always the foremost and most formidable.

However, as it often is with the obsessions of one's youth, what once inspired horror soon became the object of a twisted fascination. As the years passed I became Constance's attentive acolyte, sitting nightly by her feet and begging her for tales of the extraordinary fairy who left copper coins under nursery bedding in exchange for human teeth.

Constance was only too eager to indulge me, stoking nightly the blazing furnace of my obsession with her rough and sordid tales. By the time the first of my milk teeth was ripped, by means of a lump of hard taffy, from the bloody rookery of my gums I was filled with febrile delight at the prospect of calling to my sleeping bedside this mystifying and unnatural creature, and signing with her that strange and sordid compact.

It was my sainted mother who thwarted me in this first attempt. Having lost the tooth in private, I had shown it to none but the great simpleton Constance, on pain of biting off her littlest finger should she betray my secret. With Constance alone as my confidant I placed the bloody shard beneath the largest of the down pillows which lay upon my bed. However, before I could partake of that sweet dream-elixir, nightly administered by Constance to propel me into peaceful slumber, my mother came weeping into my bedchamber. She had been alerted by some modicum of servant's gossip to what I was attempting. With a violence of temper I had never before perceived in her, she pulled up the pillows from my bed to reveal that unclaimed tooth, resting in its gum of blood upon the crisp, white bedding.

"She calls to him," I heard Constance declare solemnly as, driven from the room, I listened for her arraignment from behind a half-closed door. "She calls to him as she called to his sister. If she doesn't have his teeth, she'll come for his soul."

The shape of her words transfixed me, though I could not comprehend their meaning.

"Not again," My mother shouted, her angelic voice rising in pitch and volume. She clutched at the small gold cross she wore habitually in the deep hollow of her delicate throat. "I'll not subject my family to any more of this madness. Leave, and take your idiot idolatry with you. There will be no more of your sorcery in this house."

Constance, her broad and homely face as bland and blank in expression as that of a cow chewing cud in a field, turned and began to walk calmly down the hallway.

I sprinted down the hall ahead of her and my mother, ducking into my own bedroom and sliding beneath the covers just as Constance entered. With a heavy gait she came up to the side of my bed. Her black silhouette looming through the bed curtain as she reached up into the canopy seemed as solid as a cliff face. Through the gap in the curtains I caught only a glimpse of what she retrieved, some talisman of polished brass, a bundle of dried herbs. She spoke in a tone as calm and steady as my mother's was animated and volatile. "You think you can drive her away with prayer, or smother his dreams with potions from the apothecary, as if that were but a different kind of witchcraft." Constance turned to me then, staring through the parted curtain at my hidden heart. She chilled me to my core...that stupid creature. She was looking into my eyes as she pronounced her final warning, "She has her hooks in him already."

"Leave," My mother shouted furiously, "Leave this house and don't ever return, you horrible woman."

And so Constance packed her meagre possessions and departed our house that very evening. As for my fallen tooth, I found out much later my mother had dissolved it in a solution of hydrofluoric acid, as she would do with all the lost teeth she procured from me during the remainder of my childhood.

"What you did is a terrible sin," She said to me later, holding my jaw so tightly in her delicate hand I feared she would break it. "You must promise, Forsythe, to never speak of the Tooth Fairy again. You mustn't call to her, nor think of her."

What could I do? I felt her love in her grip on my hand, in her fear, her wan face bright like some furious angel. "Yes, Mother," I heard myself speak, "I promise."

Had I ever intended to keep my word? Or was it, from its inception, the promise of a crocodile? I am afraid I no longer recall, for the mania had become too deeply entrenched within my psyche to be dissolved by even the potent corrosive of a mother's love.

With my own baby teeth carefully monitored and collected by my mother and the remainder of our loyal staff, I soon sought other means to procure those tokens by which I may purchase contact with the object of my unhealthy obsession.

Robbed of the abject companionship of my dear simple Constance, I took into my confidence my cousin Augusta, the daughter of an impoverished relation who was accustomed to spending summers with my mother and I. A gauche, gawky child of uniquely unattractive aspect and temperament, Augusta nevertheless held a strange fascination for me. I believe its origin lay in the extraordinary width of her jaw, like that of a grown man grafted onto the face of a child. Wary of another betrayal, I ensured Augusta's silence by means of the careful application of blackmail. Augusta was the daughter of a disgraced, insane uncle and a village prostitute, accusations against whom my sainted mother was always more than ready to believe.

As I had recalled from Constance's stories, the meaner and less erudite amongst my age-group were pledged to the Fairy less for reasons of rapt fascination, having amongst them little capacity for advancement in their understanding of the greater truths of the universe, than for purposes of crass greed. The customary price for a plebeian child's tooth, I was soon to discover, was less than one hundredth in value of my weekly allowance. It was no difficult thing, thereby, to undermine the Fairy's claim by simply topping her price. I used Augusta as my agent in this venture, her coarse upbringing affording her the freedom, in my mother's view, to associate with those whose companionship would sully a pedigree such as mine. I had her pay each child generously for their teeth, and in no time at all had amassed a collection worthy of the Tooth Fairy herself.

What a nervous wreck I must have seemed, on that fateful night when I again attempted contact. I prepared for bed in a state of extreme agitation, grateful that none but my beggared cousin were present to witness my discomposure. Yet for Augusta's part, she seemed oddly apprehensive, lingering in my bedroom far longer than was customary. I wondered if she hoped we would conspire together, whispering late into the night as we had oft done the summer before.

I was eager to get on with it, and had little regard for her presence as I prepared myself for what I had come to call 'my experiment'.

I checked beneath my pillow at least a dozen times, adjusting the position of the tooth and making sure it wasn't likely to fall or get lost in the blankets or pillowcases. I had spent some time selecting it, and I was positive it was the largest and the most healthy amongst those which Augusta had purchased for me. I'd even cleaned and polished it, a ridiculous pretension and one I never bothered with again. For all of my enthusiasm, however, I was still possessed of such astuteness as to equip myself with an ivory-handled hunting knife, an heirloom of my late father's, which I kept sheathed and belted beneath my nightclothes.

As Augusta watched all this with a strange and thoughtful eye, she had in her hand a brass coin which she passed idly across her bony knuckles in the manner of a gypsy trickster. The display was oddly captivating and even from my fervent preparations, I found myself distracted. Though the trick was beneath me, I was envious of her strange talent, and the envy quickly turned to annoyance.

"What's that?" I asked.

She didn't answer, continuing the trick in silence for a moment without looking at me. Then, in a tentative manner which was at odds with her characteristic bluntness, she asked, "Forsythe, are you sure about this?"

"What do you mean?" I replied curtly. I had been waiting so long for this night, I was impatient with any distraction.

Wordlessly, she flipped the coin across the back of one hand and made it vanish. "Have you ever wondered what a fairy would even want with your teeth?"

The question blindsided me, for in fact I hadn't wondered at all, and didn't feel much inclined to discuss the matter. I wanted desperately to sleep, but feared my anticipation was too great and I would lie awake all night, rendering my experiment a failure.

"You think I should be afraid?" I asked indignantly, even as I shoved my hands beneath my legs to hide how much they were shaking. "I'm no stupid orphan quivering in terror of the devil."

Augusta only stared at me, her expression bearing the same empty judgement as a stone icon carved on some primitive isle.

Our small parliament was soon broken up by my new governess: an owlish, aloof woman lately hired to replace Constance. Although, she spent enough time reading alone in the library that I was prone to forget I even had a governess. She herded Augusta back to her own room before returning to hastily feed me a spoonful of soothing syrup, for which I was exceedingly grateful.

That night, I dreamed of an exquisite beauty beyond the capacity of a waking mind to conceive. Crystalline turrets pierced a sky of aquatic turquoise, while oceans burned crimson with heavenly fire, darkened by the purloined light of capsized stars. I soared through the empyreal sky on wings of majesty and fire. I touched the flat of my palm to floating bubbles that appeared as lustrous as blown glass, yet were pliant and silken to the touch. And which, when slashed with my father's hunting knife, expelled a mist of such glittering grandeur its substance could be naught but grated diamond. In my mortal ears rang that celestial music of which all terrestrial melodies are a pallid imitation. I heard sounds of such lyric and melodic complexity and beauty, the like of which such pale human geniuses as Mozart or Beethoven may only aspire to compare.

Through this dreamscape I soared, over gleaming castles of burnished and bejewelled beauty, pillared cathedrals of jade and agate. I flew amongst pterosaurs and blazing phoenixes, over rolling emerald hills upon which pranced white unicorns and noble centaurs paying me gentle tribute in the quaint, pastoral manner of their kind. I swam with dolphins and merfolk alike, fought kraken and piratical phantasms. I feasted with kings and queens of ancient civilizations and visited far flung futures wherein man had evolved beyond the need for flesh and dirt, and lived eternal lives as glittering beams of purest thought.

I awoke at dawn, weeping for the beauty of all I had purchased for the price of a peasant's bicuspid. So beguiled was I, so lost in reverie, that I may not have looked beneath my pillow at all except at Augusta's insistence. What I found there was a gleaming circle of copper, not unlike the one

Augusta had shown me the night before. It was smoothly polished on one side, on the other tarnished and inscribed with four intersecting lines forming something like a sunburst, with a strange glyph carved at the apex of each of its rays. I passed the coin to Augusta, who stared at it for far longer than I ever cared to, transfixed by its ruddy gleam. In truth, I had no interest in the common bequests of the fairy kingdom. It was the otherworld I craved. Rapture, revelation, that glimpse beyond the veil.

And if my sweet Augusta voiced another warning, if she professed some sympathetic terror of what she perceived in my eyes I gave it little enough care that her words are now lost to me. The next night I returned to the dream-world of the Fairy. How could I not? How, I ask, could a young and vulnerable mind such as mine hope to have escaped such a temptation as that which faced me that night, and all those nights which followed.

In the wake of this first venture, that sweet beast of madness which had long been dogging my steps finally caught me and closed its jaws around my tender throat. I drank deep of the Fairy's dreamland. I became lost. I became an absence, naught but a host for my dreams. The torn and tepid world to which I daily returned became pallid and diseased. Food disgusted me. People irritated me. All music seemed to me the same dull drone, all colours those of a sepia-toned Hell.

Watched over by an increasingly harried Augusta, my true life I lived at night, amongst aeons of infinite grandeur, dark starlight and cosmic majesty.

My memories of this time are fragmented, at best. Days and weeks bleed together into dim obscurity, punctured by fragments of agony and ecstasy. I recall the concern of my mother, her pained voice echoing distantly from a place where she could not reach me. I recall her gathering panic, and the learned doctors called weekly into our home, the tests and questions I endured with sleepy indifference.

For all her admonishments, Augusta proved herself a devoted acolyte. She guarded my secret with a cunning and fervour which belied her lacklustre upbringing.

When my stockpile of teeth began to dwindle, I sent Augusta to the village with fistfuls of the copper coins the Fairy had left for me, tokens to which I ascribed little value. I lived only for my nightly voyages.

It was to my horror and outrage, however, that Augusta returned from the village empty-handed. It seemed that the local children, clannish and superstitious creatures by nature, had come to view me as some manner of demon. This primitive suspicion, such as it was, had finally grown sufficient in the past weeks to overcome their avarice and they had closed ranks against me, barring Augusta from their midst.

I would have taken pliers to my own jaw in a heartbeat, such was my desperation for the dreamland, had it not been for my mother's diurnal inspections of my mouth. Though it had been months since Constance's dismissal, my mother still maintained a strict regime of investigation into the state of my milk teeth. Any gap found in my gums would be a clue as to the true nature of my nightly excursions and apparent illness.

In desperation, I made attempts to be prudent with the teeth I had remaining, but each night spent on this base Earth was a night in perdition, and soon I had only one undersized, cracked and grossly stained tooth left.

This final offering I placed beneath my pillow on the eve of my eighth birthday, feeling as forlorn and dejected as I had ever felt.

For weeks I was neither truly asleep nor awake. I grasped often at hallucinations through which my pale hand passed unaffected, or else collided with things corporeal, walls and porticoes, not realizing I walked the waking world. It was in this state that I lay, my head sunk deep into the pillow, when the Tooth Fairy finally showed herself

to me.

She had white skin like smoked glass, and

was clothed in gossamer and moonlight. Six sets of

iridescent wings grew from her upper arms and

formed rainbow arches behind a head crowned

with gold and carved bone. Her long limbs and

neck recalled the style of the mannerist painters,

exquisite beauty beyond the bonds of

reality—inhuman because it is perfect, perfect

because it is inhuman. She was so tall the turrets of

her diadem would have scraped the ceiling, were she

not ethereal, and thus not bound by the laws of

matter in space. Her eyes were intersecting spirals

of colour and light which saw into my deepest heart

as even God could not. The topmost set of her

wings, glittering golden, arched backwards to cover

the lower part of her face, obscuring her mouth: the only part of herself she kept hidden from me.

I wept, then, out of lust and terror and joy. I wept as a child who perceived eternity and could not bear it.

How does one describe elation but to say that from that moment on the need for her eclipsed all human desires, all human wants and passions. It was the only true happiness I had ever, or have ever known.

When morning came I returned to this pallid human realm, and the last of the teeth I had collected was gone, replaced once again by a circle of polished copper that seemed to wink at me mockingly, in the harsh light of day.

Of what happened next, my memory is vague and incomplete. They say I attacked Augusta with lineman's pliers, beating her about the head with their grip and trying to force their steel head into her mouth, all the while hollering in some chthonian tongue no one who witnessed was able to understand. Augusta fought like a cat, I am told. I wear the mark of her teeth on my left index finger to this very day. A brutish stable hand we called Griff was summoned to separate us, for my mania was such that my mother feared for her own safety should she intercede. I recall the stink of the stable on the brute as he restrained me, his furred arms like those of a circus bear. The stink of his sweat and breath would have compounded my humiliation, had I been sane enough to care for such a thing as honour. To be lashed down by one's own servants is an affront to dignity no young man of any stature should have to face. But lashed I was, and fed a sedative through a baby's spoon feeder, until the doctors came.

Augusta was summarily shipped back to her degenerate father in their coastal shack, while I was to spend the next twelve weeks in a 'rest home' called Cosset Hill, where I was treated for my 'mania' with the learned and compassionate application of regular doses of electricity and submersions in ice water.

I had little care for the indignities of the hospital, the brutish orderlies, the chemical stench of the pale grey room to which I was confined. From the infinite cosmic majesty of the dreamland, that dull and colourless Hell became the width and breadth of my universe. My days were a mute and meaningless blur of grey, my nights as black, and deep, and empty as the grave.

It was with unparalleled joy, during one rare night of clarity within the horrid blur of my confinement, that I discovered one of my last remaining milk teeth had become loose. Though doubly bound to my bed and garmented in a canvas straightjacket I managed, with much patience and protracted worrying with my tongue, to wrench the tooth free and manoeuvre myself into position to spit it beneath my pillow, confident that one more bloodstain upon the hospital linen would not stand out amongst the others.

But the Fairy did not visit me in the hospital. Perhaps it was the vigilance of the learned doctors who kept her away. Or else it was such a bleak and dreary place that, even for the edification of such a desperate wretch as she had made me into, she would not demean herself to enter.

When the tooth was discovered beneath my pillow I was brought before the head of the hospital as a prisoner to the gallows. The eminent Doctor Mikhail Kozlov, a broad and barbarous creature with the continence less of a man than of a learned ape, sat at a large and polished desk before which I was deposited by a pair of goonish orderlies. His thick fingers were steepled in some parody of thought as he hummed and hawed to himself and studied me.

"You are resisting treatment," he told me, his words garbled beyond sense by his ridiculous accent.

"I am resistant to your absurdity," I said, "I am resisting torture."

"You believe we are torturing you?" said the crafty ape, "We are healers here, Mr. Ward."

"You are barbarians," I hissed, speaking in a voice that was not my own. "Return my tooth to me or burn in Hell." It was as if some distant entity were speaking through me. I had lost all control. I ran my tongue across the bloody gap in my gums, and the sharp, tiny teeth that still resided there. I had only twelve of my milk teeth left, though none of my adult teeth had yet come in to replace them. Most of the food in the hospital being served in the form of a nutritional slurry, this had so far not proved particularly vexing.

"Of course," said the learned creature, studying me impassively with the vague, cruel eyes of a reptile, "This obsession with teeth is the most damaging. They are the focal point of all of his delusions. We must remove the source of his fixation if we are to commence with the healing. The means may seem drastic, punitive, even cruel. But I assure you, Mrs. Ward, it is absolutely necessary."

Mrs. Ward, I realized suddenly that Doctor Kozlov had stopped talking to me some time ago. I strained against the restrictions of my straightjacket to turn my head. My sainted mother, gaunter than she had lately been, and reddened around the eyes, stood behind me, dressed in a stiff gown of so uncharacteristically dark a shade it was as close as was socially permissible to a mourning gown. Had she dressed herself in simulated mourning for a still living child? Was I, in my madness, so dead to her? I remember so little of my time in the asylum, but the feeling of my heart breaking.

She wept softly into a handkerchief, and did not look at me. "Do what you must, Doctor," she said, "I implore you, do what is necessary."

Dissolving into animal screams, I was dragged through the sanitized glare of the hallways to a room with a large metal chair in its centre, rooted to the tiled floor. I was strapped down into this chair, arms and legs bound. The chair was then lowered and tilted back so I had no view but that of the harsh ceiling lights and needlepoints of black as they seared my vision. A leather strap was fastened across my forehead, a rubber bit forced into my mouth. I saw the face of the dental surgeon: disembodied, monstrous, hovering above mine. And though his mouth was completely covered by a stiff white surgical mask, I knew in my gut that he was smiling. As his skeletal fingers pressed into my gums I could taste the rubber of his gloves, and feel them, wet and slick like the body of an eel against my tongue. Helpless, jaws forced apart, I could not use my precious twelve teeth to bite that hand and rend it bloody, however badly I wanted to. Such was the madman I had become.

When he brought the gleaming jaws of the surgical pliers up to my mouth I screamed from the hollow of my throat, the sound rendered subhuman by the objects stuffed into my mouth. As he wretched from my jaw every last one of my deciduous teeth the spasms of pain, and the blood filling the back of my throat, were meaningless compared to the bleak knowledge of what I had truly lost. Not only my hope of ever experiencing the dreamland again, but all I had sacrificed in its pursuit: my dignity, my sanity, the adoration of my sainted mother. I wept, then, as blood and saliva dribbled down my chin and soaked coldly into the off-white canvas of my straight jacket, and there was nothing I could do to wipe it away. I wept as I had never wept before, a creature truly and profoundly broken.

Part II:

An Obsession Reignited

Dr. Kozlov may have been more than the deplorable savage I had initially supposed, for as my adult teeth began to grow in, so began my slow return to sanity. Little by little, the call of the Dreamland began to recede from my consciousness, as true nightmares do with time. My memories of those trials and humiliations I had faced began to feel like a terrible dream from which I had finally awakened.

I returned to my family's manor for two weeks in the summer following my eighth birthday. Though I still craved my mother's presence on an instinctual level, for the base comfort it afforded me even now, I saw little of her in this time. She was remote, often confined to her room, and when we did cross paths she hardly spoke to me except to repeat those empty platitudes with which one might greet a distant acquaintance run into by accident upon a train platform, just before boarding. In point of fact, the most clear and meaningful communication she deigned to afford her only son at this troubled time was this: she continued to favour dark dresses, as she would until the end of her life.

The servants, as well, had become obviously discomforted by my presence around my old home. They spoke to me only as much as required, and contrived to slip unnoticed from rooms that I had recently entered. It became disturbingly clear, as the weeks passed, that I could not linger at Ivory Oak Manner, for the estate had become haunted to me now, and it was increasingly clear to me that the ghost which haunted it was myself.

Therefore, less than a month after my release from that odious institution at Cosset Hill, I boarded a train to the Miskatonic Academy for boys, the first in a series of prestigious boarding schools where I was to spend the majority of my adolescence. I returned to Ivory Oak manner, a place no paroxysm of sentiment could anymore induce me to refer to as my home, for exactly two weeks each Christmas, and four weeks of every summer. For all lesser holidays I remained housed at whichever palace of learning I was currently matriculating, haunting its esteemed hallways as a phantom, eminent in my loneliness and the hallowed dust of decades.

During those rare visits to my ancestral 'home' my mother remained distant to me, greeting me coldly when I arrived. Whenever I walked into a room she was currently occupying, she seemed to look up at me with some shadow of deep alarm on her delicate features, as if I were not the son she had raised but some apparition appearing suddenly in the night. The long bouts of silence that stretched between us were punctuated, with increasing frequency as I grew to manhood, by a sharp cough. It was a pert and delicate cough at first, stifled quite gracefully by the silk handkerchief embroidered with dandelions that she carried with her always. But as the years passed the cough became more pronounced. Our quiet visits were often pervaded upon by deluges of hacking which forced my mother to remove herself from company and retire early to her bedroom with a hot water bottle and a teaspoon of laudanum. Often, the yellow dandelions that edged her handkerchief bloomed amongst rosebuds of dark blood.

I was twenty years old, in my third year of study at the prestigious Eibon University, when I received a telegram from Mr. Simon Smith, our family lawyer, informing me that my mother had finally succumbed to her long illness and had been pronounced dead in the early hours of that morning. I was to return to Ivory Oak at once to attend her funeral, and to see to the matter of her internment in the family crypt. At this juncture, I had not spoken to my mother, nor set foot on the grounds of Ivory Oak, in over three years.

I returned to my childhood home to find it a bleak and dismal place, most of the rooms closed off, and the furniture covered. My mother had lived the life of a recluse in her final years, attended in her deterioration by my old nurse Constance. The old ox had been reengaged on some sentimental whim of my mother's, as the tide of her life ebbed and her mental facilities, no doubt, began to fail her.

My mother, it seemed, had begun to suffocate in the night and had been ringing Constance's bell to summon the woman to her aid. In the late stage of her illness my mother had been subject to intermittent cessations of her breathing and had required constant vigilance on the part of her attendants. The old nurse had been rushing to my mother's bedside when she had lost her footing on the grand staircase in the foyer and tumbled all the way to the ground floor, where she cracked her skull on the final step.

Without Constance to administer to her needs, my mother had choked to death on her own disintegrating lungs. She was found the following morning by the same young maid who had, mere minutes earlier, discovered the twisted corpse of Constance on the foyer floor and whom, I am assured, was summarily traumatized by the entire ordeal.

How I loathed Constance then, for it was twice over that she had robbed me of my mother: once of her love, and now of her life. So you will understand my consternation when I was met at the gates to my old home by an oversized ape of a man, bearing the same dull countenance I recalled so well from my childhood. He presented his thick, meaty paw to me and informed me that his name was Hamish, and that he was Constance's son, hired by Mr. Smith as caretaker at Ivory Oak Manor. Perhaps due to some sentimental stirrings of my own, however, I did not dismiss him out of hand. My mother lived a solitary existence in her final years, and I did not fancy troubling myself to procure replacements for the small staff she had chosen to keep with her until the end.

My mother's funeral was a small and lonely affaire. Mr. Smith was in attendance, along with Hamish, and my old playmate Augusta, looking cold and severe in a plain, unflattering dress with a high collar that only accentuated her deformed jaw. Her teeth, I noticed on those few occasions when she was not hiding them beneath a baleful scowl, were as white as ocean pearls. That she had travelled to Ivory Oak alone, her father's drunken disgrace allied with her own ugliness and distemper leaving her a confirmed spinster at twenty-one, came as no surprise to me. We each still wore the scars we had given to one another. However, her presence still did its work to displace some small particle of the desolation which had filled me since my return, and for that she had my gratitude, if not my love. The service was held in the family chapel: swept and dusted for the occasion, as well as evacuated of rats, racoons and other vermin it had played host to over the years. The congregation of four was presided over by a minister from the village, who recited dull sermons for the benefit of deaf ears. I had seen what lay beyond this veil of tears, and though I remained ignorant of its true purpose, I knew enough to call it neither peace nor salvation. From the cast of Augusta's gaze, I knew she understood the same dark truth as I.

With the business of my mother's death reaching its conclusion, I made no plans to return to Eibon to resume my education. I could not place

why, but something in my childhood home seemed

to call to me, pulling me irrevocably towards its

unexplored centre. Despite the swift delivery of my

mother's remains to their proper resting place

alongside my father, something about my journey

here felt unfinished. I languished at Ivory Oak,

spending my days wandering its dusty hallways

filled with dangerous longing. I had such dreams

then, as I had not had since I was a child. Not the

glories of the Fairy's Dreamland, you understand,

for such rapture had long been lost to me, but

echoes of the night terrors which had preceded that

first obsession. In all the nightmares that plagued

me during this time, there seemed to be one central

theme. I saw a spectre of a book, handwritten and

bound in dark leather, its thick cover bearing a

curious imprint of human teeth, as if it had been repeatedly bitten. When I took the book from the hands of whatever faceless being had presented it to me, I found the words it contained were indecipherable, written in a language no mortal being could comprehend.

In a state of vexation, I visited Mr. Smith in his offices and implored him to tell me if he recalled seeing a book such as the one I described in my mother's possession, or in the hands of any of the servants while he had been at Ivory Oak manor attending to her affaires. A look of consternation passed over his meek and nebbish face as he attempted to dissuade me from perusing this subject. I persisted, however, and eventually was met with capitulation.

"Your mother willed it to be burned, you understand," he stammered at me, his rattish whiskers quivering absurdly. "But she had no legal power to do so. It was left in trust, for you, by your great uncle."

"I don't have a great uncle," I said.

"I assure you Master Ward," said Mr. Smith, "You do. Edmond Forsythe Ward: you were named for him. Surely your mother mentioned him?"

I gave him the blackest of stares, and he moved on from the topic. "He was something of a black sheep, I'm given to understand. A lifelong bachelor, there were rumours about him."

"What sort of rumours?" I demanded.

The lawyer's face darkened, "All sorts of rumours," he said, "That he was mad, cursed, involved in the occult. The former was proven at least partially accurate in the end. He died by his own hand: shot himself twice in the face."

"Twice?" I asked, looking sharply down into the diminutive lawyer's pale, watery eyes.

A nervous cough of laughter, quickly smothered, "Oh no, nothing funny about it I assure you. He used a matching set of duelling pistols, fired one with either hand, both into his own mouth. He must have been mighty sure of himself is all I can say, as well as...what's the word?"

"Ambidextrous?" I suggested.

"Indeed," the lawyer confirmed.

"You had no legal right to keep my property from me," I said coldly, "And that's exactly what you did. What do you suggest I take from that?"

His runtish face began to quiver again, and he wrung his limp little hands at me. "Your mother was a good woman," he said finally, "I cared for her deeply. Unable as I was to adhere to her other, final request, I only meant to act in accordance with her wishes. It was nothing of value that was kept from you, you understand, only an old diary and...remnants of madness. Your mother was so adamant..."

"I wish to have it," I told him.

"I implore you, for your mother's sake, to reconsider."

I remained unswayed by the executor's prattle. "It is my legal right."

Defeated, Mr. Smith acquiesced, and brought from a locked cabinet behind his desk a rusted steel box, like an old sea trunk with its hasp long rotted away.

I placed the box down on the desk and opened it, flakes of red rust falling off of it and collecting upon the lawyer's papers. Inside, bound and bitten exactly as I had seen it in my dreams, was a book: the lost diary of my uncle Edmond Forsythe Ward. I opened the book to the first page, and saw a long and spidery hand. They were the ramblings of a madman, perhaps, but ramblings recorded in unmistakably plain and proper English.

However, before I could return to Ivory Oak Manor to delve with utmost enthusiasm into the esoteric scrawling of my deranged uncle, there was one final question I could not help but ask.

"You said you were unable to adhere to my mother's final request," I said, without looking up from my uncle's handwriting, "What exactly was that request?"

"I...I thought you knew," the lawyer stammered, "She was not herself, in the end. What she wanted: it would have been a desecration."

"What-" I asked once again, "-was her final request?"

"Your mother," the man stated dumbly, an aura of loathsome defeat surrounding him like a stench, "Requested that the teeth be pulled from her corpse before she was laid to rest."

I nodded solemnly, to the lawyer's utmost dismay, having expected nothing else.

Part III:
The Diary of Edmond Forsythe Ward

January 15, 18--

I had the dream again last night. Blood spilling out of my mouth, torrents of it overflowing my cupped hands and pooling on the floor, my bare feet sliding on puddles of my own blood. Pursued across the aeons by some rough beast I cannot see nor fathom, always just behind, it's breath between my shoulders, spearing my heart.

I think back on my youth and wonder if I was ever so innocent. The years have brokered a descent into such an abattoir as I cannot escape. And I know that I am damned. Such lows I have sunk to that the commonplace mind may not even imagine. What miser would deny me pity, though, for the Tooth Fairy has consumed my soul.

I looked up from my uncle's untidy hand, aghast. Edmond Ward knew of the Fairy! Had he courted her, as I had? Had he placed teeth, his own or those procured, beneath his pillow and walked with her through that same celestial grandeur which had brought me such early misery? I had to know! I read on.

February 28, 18--

I have been down to the crypt. I tried to resist. God help me I tried to resist! I have defiled them: the corpses of children, doll-like in their infinite rest. I have debased myself. But still, my ethereal mistress refuses me. She wants me to suffer, to be punished for my unworthiness. I cannot bear it! If I am to be barred forever from her sight, I shall not permit myself to survive. I shall take myself to the highest tower of Ivory Oak Manor, and hurl myself into whatever black abyss awaits me. On my soul I swear.

I flipped ahead through the brittle pages, skimming over entry after entry. There were deranged ramblings, yes, lamentations, litanies of warnings for future generations, as well as detailed descriptions of dreams and hallucinations such as contested any lingering doubt that my uncle had been an utter madman in his final years. Yet betwixt these anguished tirades there were also maps, drawings, travelogues, carefully kept records of scientific inquiry.

Impulsively, I flipped ahead to the very end of the book, hoping for some final conclusion...

March 10, 18--

I have met a mystic in the far reaches of the world, a charlatan perhaps, but I have nothing but my fortune left to lose and that, in itself, is worthless to me. He claims he can propel me into that state I knew as a child, that state in which I may perceive my ethereal mistress once again. The means are dangerous, and necessitate a level of personal abasement and moral depravity such as I dare not record here. On that subject I shall write only this: If I were not damned from that first night in my youth when I slept with a lost molar beneath my pillow, I should surely be damned tonight.

It was at this point that I hurled the diary to the floor in anger. How could my uncle not have recorded his discovery? How could he deny me that knowledge which I craved with every modicum of my soul? Was I to remain forever on this plain, mired in the offal of plodding banality? It was then that I finally admitted to myself that which I had only previously known in dreams: my time in the asylum had never truly cured me. I was an obsessive still, and freely so. I would follow in my damned uncle's footsteps if it led me to naught but my own death and ruination, or else my life would peter away, incomplete. I picked up the book again and turned to the final page of the diary, a fine dust of ash falling from between the yellowed pages and drifting down to the ground.

Date Unknown, 18--

Whoever should find this diary after I am dead, let this be a warning unto thee: tread not the road I have walked, for it is paved with bone, blood, and most of all, teeth.. I have known horrors which no mortal man was meant to know. I have perceived the end of this universe, the death and degradation of all living things. It is knowledge from which there is no escape but that which lies in madness or death. Tonight I shall condemn myself to Hell, for no punitive ministration which may be visited upon me by the Christian Devil holds any terror for me now, I have known a far worse Hell than that.

Before I commit the final sin of self-slaughter, I will gather all the specimens I have collected and destroy them. I have committed them to the flames, but they will not burn. God save me, THEY WILL NOT BURN.

I dipped my hand into the steel chest in which the diary had been kept and found what I had at first mistaken for flakes of rust were in fact fragments of human teeth, burnt and blackened from the fires of Uncle Edmond's madness. It seemed that when the fires had failed him, he had resorted to smashing what was left of the teeth to pieces with a hammer, or some other blunt instrument.

I placed the book back into the box and hid it in my childhood bedroom, then I called for Hamish.

"What can I do for you, sir?" Hamish asked, as pleasant and docile as a friendly sheepdog.

"We're going to visit the family crypt, Hamish," I said to him, "It's time I fulfilled my mother's final request."

Hamish lit a torch, and side by side we walked down into the stone-walled catacomb of my kindred dead, lighting the wall sconces each as we passed, filling the hallways with macabre shadows that danced like skeletal bacchae in the thrall of pandemonic frenzy.

This crypt in which the most esteemed of my ancestors had been entombed inspired little of the awe and reverence it once had. Now I saw naught but a house of decay, a monument to the decrepitude of ages past.

"If I am ever entombed here," I said aloud, "Let my true home be in Hell."

Hamish looked at me when I said this, as if to venture a word. Wisely, he stopped his blabbing mouth, and turned away. I was in no mood for a servant's prattle. A rat scurried across our path, and for a moment it was the only sound that existed in all the plains and expanses of the megacosm, from the deepest reaches of space to the most sinister depths of the human heart.

I walked up to one of the carved stone sarcophagi and ran my fingers across the inscription, etched in tarnished bronze: *Forsythe Augustine Ward III*. Atop the lid of the sarcophagus was a stone rendering of an angel, prostrated in mourning with its face turned to one side, wings skewed at odd angles as if broken. I circled the casket, taking the torch from Hamish's meaty paw as I ascended the stone steps to cast its meagre glow on the angel's sorrow-pinched visage.

I gasped, and nearly dropped the torch. It was my mother's face, unquestionably, though twisted and made hideous in mourning.

"It's a beautiful tribute," stammered Hamish stupidly, "Your parents must have loved each other very much."

"One wonders at the sculptor's competence," I said, "He's made her look more demon than angel. Only a fool could call such a thing beautiful."

Again some sentiment of buffoonery stopped itself on the edge of Hamish's tongue, and again I was glad of it.

"Help me move it," I said.

Hamish looked around dumbly, I know not what for. "I'm sorry sir, but move what?"

"This lid, of course, it's too heavy to move on my own."

"But your mother was laid to rest there," he said, pointing to the smooth, white marble box that lay alongside my father's casket.

"I know that, you idiot. I want to open this one."

"Why, sir?"

"Never mind why," I told the great brute, "Just do what I tell you."

Dumbly, the oaf braced his boat-like feet on the bottommost step of the podium upon which my father's casket lay. His thick arms tensed and he grunted like a feeding hog as he pushed the lid of the sarcophagus, revealing the lacquered surface of my father's coffin.

I stood on the top step of the podium, wedged the torch between the angel's broken wings and slowly lifted the gilt edged lid of the interior coffin. At that moment, I felt nothing. My obsession was no respecter of grief or horror. But years later, as I wandered the earth like a vagabond, in pursuit of my own doom, I would often be woken in the night by the phantom stench of my father's decay. Carefully, I parted the grey shreds of my father's shroud. Cobwebs and leather-like strips of flesh clung to the rotten cloth, I coughed repeatedly as the dust of old death filled my lungs.

Finally the naked skull was revealed. I reached into the coffin and ran the tip of my finger along the curved length of his perforated jaw. In the absolute absence of teeth, his skull did not look to be grinning as unclothed skulls are wont to do, but instead seemed to be screaming its way through eternity. Had my mother come down to this crypt and wrenched out his teeth herself, I wondered idly, with her own small and delicate hands? Had she dissolved her husband's most immortal parts in caustic acid as she had her son's?

"I must open another," I said to Hamish, "Any other."

"Why?" Hamish mewed, a coward despite his copious size.

I turned my head from the sight of my father's caterwauling corpse and looked Hamish in the eye. "You cannot imagine," I said slowly, punctuating every word so that the simpleton might understand, "How sick to death I am of hearing you ask me that." I stood firm, brushed the grave dust off my coat, and plucked the torch from between the angel's wings. "We'll uncover my grandmother," I decided.

I stepped down from the podium and circled the crypt, casting the torchlight upon the tarnished nameplates of my esteemed ancestors. Behind me, I heard the sound of stone scraping on stone mingled with the undignified grunts of my serving man as he struggled to straighten the lid of my father's sarcophagus.

"No," I said, considering every variable as I searched through the catacombs, "My grandmother was old, likely to have lost her teeth naturally. It has to be someone who died young."

"There," I pointed with the head of the torch towards the box I wanted opened. My hand shook with apprehension, making the torchlight dance upon the brass nameplate. Honoria Ward, a distant cousin who'd been strangled by her betrothed at the age of twenty-five. Placing the torch in an empty wall sconce, I stepped up to her casket.

"Come here, you moron," I said to Hamish. The brute seemed to hesitate a moment, but quickly came to heel alongside Honoria's sarcophagus. Together we shoved aside the lid to reveal the lacquered pink lid surface of her coffin. Hastily, I lifted the lid of the second box and took stock of its contents.

Like my father, my cousin Honoria had been laid to rest without a single tooth in her skull. Why? Had it been her will? An obscure and macabre family tradition that had somehow escaped my hearing? Or had she been robbed of her teeth after death by some demon or deranged scavenger? Perhaps I shall die without ever knowing the true depth of my family's entanglement with the Tooth Fairy. But one fact was clear: I was not the first soul at Ivory Oak to have been visited by the Tooth Fairy, nor was I the first to have admired and feared her in equal measures. I had known already, of course, that as an irrefutable suicide my Uncle Edmond would have been denied internment here. It was a custom my family adhered to out of necessity as much as tradition, for without it the tomb would have long-ago become overcrowded.

In the absence of his corpse to scrutinize, I recalled instead what my great uncle had inscribed in his diary: *I have defiled them: the corpses of children.*

I called to my servant over the horrid screeching of Honoria's heavy stone sarcophagus lid being shoved back into place. "Come, Hamish," I said, seizing our torch and holding it aloft. "This way."

I forged quickly ahead, forcing Hamish to keep pace with me. I was led, as if by the pull of some apparitional string, to that sad room swarmed by fat cherubim and mewling seraphs, where the children had been laid to rest.

Hamish looked about the room with his idiot's eyes, empty of everything but the reflection of the torchlight. His base, over-wide mouth twisted into strange shapes, but thankfully, no words emerged.

It had been more than a decade since I had ventured down this far, yet I found my sister's tomb with hardly a conscious thought. Sweet Antigone had been laid to rest in a diminutive casket of polished white marble, carved with a relief of prancing unicorns.

"This one," I told Hamish. "Open it."

"Sir..." Hamish said.

"Open it, I said."

"No sir, I won't."

I turned my head to regard Hamish, standing oafishly in the arched doorway, his flame-sharpened shadow falling across a relief of Saint Michael wrestling a dragon.

"What did you say?"

"I won't sir," he said, "I'm sorry. I won't."

"Fine," I replied, too absorbed by my investigation to be bothered with upbraiding a presumptuous servant. Antigone's casket was small, and I could push aside its lid easily enough on my own.

Hamish watched, slack-jawed and gaping, as I undressed Antigone's small, smooth skull and ran my finger along the length of her jawbone. Did I imagine it, or was the scent of rot tinged with some remnant of the rose and ambergris which had killed her?

Her teeth were gone. Was it my mother's handiwork? Had she defiled her own daughter's corpse in her effort to save us all from the Tooth Fairy's enthrallment? Or did someone else amongst my kinfolk share my passion?

And then I spied a thing which nearly stopped the heart in my chest. It appeared as if by providence, for I swear it had not been there a moment before: a single, pearly molar. It was small, malformed and impacted, stuck deep in the jawbone.

"Pliers, Hamish," I said, sticking out my hand.

"What do you intend to do?" He asked.

"No questions, Hamish," I said, not taking my eyes off of the tooth, "The pliers."

Hamish moved closer to the casket, his steps heavy and slow.

"Quickly, you buffoon," I said.

"Come down from there, sir," he said slowly. He seemed to be speaking to me in a primitive dialect which bore some resemblance to proper English, yet was utterly alien to civilized ears. I recognised the words, but their arrangement was utterly indecipherable. "You're in a state of grief," said the great moron, "All the darkness and downright eeriness down here has gotten into your head, and you're set to do something you'll regret. Please, sir, leave your poor sister to her rest."

"What do you know about anything you imbecile?" I demanded, stepping down from the podium and putting out my hand, "Give me the pliers."

The brute didn't relent. "You've lost your mum," he said, "I've lost mine too, so I can understand how grief can make you not quite yourself..."

Rage began to boil in my heart, cutting through the icy cold of the tomb. "You will not speak about my mother," I yelled at him, that arrogant slave I'd pitied and granted refuge in my home despite the legacy of degenerate filth from which he had sprung, "You will never compare *my* mother to that odious slag from whose decrepit

cunt you crawled..."

A sickening crack echoed through the tomb

as his meaty paw slammed into my face. I tumbled

backwards onto the stone steps of Antigone's

podium, a field of white stars sparkling in front of

my face. I could taste the coppery tang of blood as it

dribbled down onto my lips from my broken nose. I

could do nothing but lay still, too stunned to move.

"Mrs. Ward's last request was strange to me

sir," Hamish said, his words coloured by a faint

regional accent I'd never noticed before. "But I've

known of a family tradition or two that may have

seemed odd to an outsider, so I was content to take

a dying lady at her word. But if you want to defile

the body of an innocent child you'll have to do it

without my help."

Perhaps I should have been more frightened than I was, menaced by that overgrown animal, a tamed beast gone rabid down there in the dark, but I had eyes only for the pair of pliers clipped to his thick, workman's belt. I staggered to my feet and leapt at him, throwing myself at his thick waist and trying to wrench the pliers free from his belt. His hand landed near my face in his attempt to dislodge my grip on his belt and I bit down on it, tasting his vulgar blood mixing with my own.

The oaf twisted his hand free of my mouth and shoved me back. The spasms of pain that followed the collision of my spine with the stone floor left me prone and breathless.

There was a weird calm in Hamish's voice when he spoke next. The heat of anger, perhaps, caused his accent to become more pronounced, though his voice remained soft and quiet.

"You were a damned monster when you were a boy," he said, "And you're a damned monster now."

He took the torch with him as he left, so I remained in the dark, sprawled on the cold steps with blood from my nose running freely and soaking into my shirt, my bruised spine screaming.

For some reason I no longer recall, I began to laugh. I went on laughing for a long, long while.

Part IV:

The Wanderer in the Dark

Constance's stories had always been rooted in the village, so that was where I began my search. I went door to door, offering silver in exchange for any spare word or whisper of commiseration. Though these simple souls had not been cursed by the Tooth Fairy's favour as I had been, they *had* made their own primitive compacts with her and received her gifts. However, no one would speak to me. Men slammed doors in my face. At best the feeble, mousy faces of their women peered at me through cracked doors, shook their heads, and mutely sent me away.

If Augusta were with me, I wondered, would they have known her? Were these the aged faces, lined and darkened by years of slavish ignorance and childrearing, of the children whose teeth I had once purchased? Their teeth were brown and broken now, with only a few boasting a full set, and therein lay the story of man's innocence.

I came soon to the realization that there was nothing to be learned in the valley. If ever there had been a door to the unseen, it was closed to me now. I must seek the empyreal through other, darker means. And so I set upon my travels.

This was the juncture upon which I ceased completely to be a man of civility and gentle birth, and became a devient—a true son of my cursed and fallen family. Fate took its own course, and with my great uncle's diary as my guide I set out to find what I found.

I closed down the house and dismissed what was left of the staff. My legal affairs I left in the hands of Mr. Smith, and took with me only a single trunk containing amongst some basic necessities: my father's knife, a pair of guns, and the diary.

I followed my doomed uncle's path across the globe, my footsteps overlaying the cartography of his damnation. Has there ever been a greater and more knowing act of self-destruction? I cannot say. I had but a single goal, and that I pursued with relentless ambition. With my uncle's broad and frenzied scribbling as my guide, I searched the world for traces of the Fairy, for any evidence of human teeth being harvested, studied or enshrined for esoteric purposes.

I travelled to the Antarctic with a scientific expedition, and viewed an ancient idol carved from the skull and tusks of a mastodon. I had hoped the primitive pictographs carved into the bones would bear some resemblance to the esoteric script I had seen in my dreams, but these letters were crude and plain: barely claw-marks on the ancient ivory.

I met with a fortune teller in a travelling carnival, who read my future in the random configurations of the fragments of a human jawbone, tossed by an arthritic hand upon a table clothed in circus silk. The gypsy grinned as he tossed the bones, showing teeth that were whiter than diamonds.

I listened to his prophecies of misery and doom with naught a stirring of apprehension, jaded and numb to the promise of any curse falling upon me but that which I had carried from my nursery like a vestigial twin.

In a small village in southern France, near the Spanish border, I was nearly mauled to death by a horde of crazed mice in an adventure far too absurd to be believed.

I perused peasant rumours, ancient legends, old wives' tales: more often than not the irrational ravings of elderly dipsomaniacs. But of my ethereal mistress? Not a whisper. And so, in my desperation, I was driven yet farther from the path of virtue, and into the realms of the truly debased.

I chased a rumour to the Italian Countryside, where there was said to live a countess who had been born with a set of perfectly formed teeth within the fleshy crevice between her legs. They were not real teeth, anymore than the woman was a real countess. Just a pretty peasant woman who'd been dressed in old carnival costumes and fitted with a porcelain prosthetic. Her family had installed her in a drafty bedroom of the abandoned castle in which they were squatting, and charged the curious or the perverse one coin to view the aberration, or three to bed it. I placed my coins in the wooden bowl by the door, and walked away.

In the bazaars of the Far East, I met mountebanks who had available for purchase, amongst the typical potions and fetishes of their deplorable trade, sacks of 'human' teeth. One of them, naught but a decrepit sack of bones himself, opened his leather sachet for me and filled my palm with a sample of his stock. Some of the teeth were clearly animal, others broken into pieces, or black with rot. Some, however, were human, and among those some were clearly from children: dark with blood, some still bound in the yellowed fragments of a jaw bone.

Did I do business with these men? Let me answer clearly: I swear that I did not. To those who would appoint themselves the arbiters of my soul, know that I had these scruples left at least. I passed through those bone markets with my soul no further blackened than it had already been.

During my travels, it had become difficult to procure the chlorodyne I was accustomed to taking for my insomnia and migraines, and I was forced to rely on strange foreign brands bearing labels that were often indecipherable to me. It was from the somnolent rapture of these anesthetized nights that I dreamed of her most vividly, perceiving her draped visage as if through a layer of fog, her form and shadow a shimmer in the dust, the shape of her departing back, the glitter trail left by a lustrous wing upon the wooden sill of a shattered window.

In Germany, mostly by way of bribery and persistence, I gained ingress amongst a secretive coven of libertines, who drove themselves to ritualistic frenzy through fetishistic acts of carnassial idolatry, calling themselves the Votary of the Fanged. At their bi-monthly bacchanals, while dressed in exotic and often obscene costumes, they would imbibe great quantities of liquor and partake of strange vapours sucked from a heavy brass tank. Then, once they had been rendered insensible through these means, they would fall amongst their fellows as animals on their hands and knees, baying in devotion to some fanged and winged goddess who bore some passing resemblance to the icon of my own heart.

The teeth of these acolytes were often sharpened and capped to resemble those of wolves or tigers. The most affluent among the cult had them embedded with precious stones. One mad soul had had installed in place of his own canines a pair of sharpened steel spikes which were liable to pierce through his own lower lip whenever he closed his mouth, leaving the lower part of his mouth a hideous ruin of scar-tissue.

They were a base and carnal lot, for the most part, debauched sensualists driven imbecilic by crude indulgence. Yet there were whispers, further secrets even amongst the irredeemably depraved, which spoke of transcendence. And wasn't it amongst these festivals of heavenly anguish and hellish ecstasy that I came nearest to feeling that celestial presence? Could the path of excess truly lead to the palace of wisdom?

I gained my answer upon one dark and foggy evening when I had partaken, in my pursuit of acclivity and truth, of some stimulating substance reputed to expand and enhance the mind's capacity for abstract thought. Wandering through the bleak hallways of the country estate upon which this particular evening's revelry was being enacted, I caught sight of a young woman dressed in one of the particular costumes favoured by the bacchants. She was a delicate creature, little more than a waif, and had the empty eyes of an idiot. Yellow-haired and pale as smoke, she danced inanely through the labyrinthine hallways of the large estate, motioning with a crooked finger for me to follow. I would have ignored her summons, of course, not being accustomed to trailing after the whims of drunken slatterns, but for the particularities of the costume she wore. She was shamelessly naked, as was typical amongst her tribe, but for a half dozen diaphanous scarves trailing from each of her arms, mimicking the form of wings. Gold, lavender, indigo, scarlet and emerald: and the two silver scarves attached near her bony shoulders, which had been drawn upwards and wrapped around the lower part of her face, obscuring her mouth.

And upon her head, worn lopsided like a pirate's bounty placed in lewd jest upon the head of his dockside whore, sat a diadem of polished ivory so like the Fairy's own crown, it could have been plucked manifest from the landscape of my own dreams.

Beguiled, I approached her. I grabbed her arm, desperately afraid she would vanish before my questions had been answered.

"Who are you?" I asked.

She responded in a drunken garble of German.

"Who told you to dress like that?" I demanded. Her arm was so thin that my grip closed completely around it. She turned, jerked forward, and focused her barren stare on my hand on her arm. Her eyes bore the colour and lustre of cooked fish flesh.

As with all truly beautiful things, proximity revealed her hidden hideousness: white skin dry and scabrous, bones protruding sickly. The lines around her eyes and mouth revealed her age, as did the spider webs of purplish veins forking down from her nose. Her neck and shoulders bore the multicoloured bruises and lacerations of various bite wounds, some still swollen and leaking yellowish puss. I peeled the silver scarf away from her face. Her thin-lipped mouth gaped like a cracked clam to reveal a row of perfect ocean pearls. She giggled insipidly, tilting back her head as if in anticipation of a kiss. Her breath stank of wormwood and curdled milk.

I wanted to turn away, incensed by the blasphemy of this all-too-mortal waif dressed in pallid mockery of my fairy goddess. It was her teeth that kept me rooted before her, grip still tight around her pale mantis arm. They were miniscule, uniformly spaced a great width apart, as if a child's first teeth had been evenly distributed and implanted within the mouth of a stunted adult. The mystery entranced me. Was she an idiot, stunted in mind and body? Her teeth simply never maturing beyond the capacity of a retarded psyche?

Or had her teeth been surgically augmented to appear thus, in the tradition of her jewelled and silver-fanged compatriots?

The stimulants I had been fed crystallized impulse into action. Her idiot flailing obliged me to brace her against a stained and graffitied wall in order to properly investigate the matter of her nature. Though her weak and undersized body made her relatively easy to subdue, her incessant antagonism further obliged me to stick a knife blade vertically into her mouth to keep her from clamping her jaw shut or trying to bite me. Her teeth were flawless, rooted, and clean of any file marks to indicate they had been whittled down into such an unlikely shape.

Did an imbecile retain the same privileges of a child? Did the Fairy visit this stunted creature in the dull desolation of her dreams, offering her transcendence like pearls thrown into a pig's trough? The notion was obscene, that this puerile dwarf should be afforded glimpses of the divine while I remained an exile.

Seized by a strange impulse I couldn't control, I drove her harder into the wall and covered her thin, wet mouth with mine. Her crown, a gaudy circlet of painted tin, clattered to the stone floor. I could feel her heartbeat quicken beneath the brittle cage of her ribs. A squeaky stream of protesting German was cut off by a sick croak, and I looked down from her deadened eyes to see my own hand tightening around a throat that could well have been constructed from hollow reeds and paper mache, so false and frail did it feel beneath my grip. She may as well have been a straw effigy, such was the impression of life she gave in that moment. She may as well have been already dead.

Gloved hands grabbed me from behind and I turned to see Diedrick, the hulking, steel-fanged creature with the mangled lip. He looked from me to the waif, conversing with her in their own barking, barbarous language.

He turned and swung at me, breaking my nose with far less force than Hamish had, but with much greater precision. At first it hardly hurt at all, and then it was agony.

Diedrick, I knew, spoke English, yet he offered me no reason or reprimand in any proper tongue; adding a deliberate insult to the beating which was to follow. He called out to his fellow cultists, "Kommen Sie hier," and they came to heel beside him. One of them was an obscenely muscular woman dressed in a whalebone corset that barely indented her brawny and fleshless torsos. Her teeth were capped with oversized daggers of yellowing ivory that were so obviously false they may as well have been formed in a plaster mold. The man with her was shirtless, his thick torso hairless and oiled, his teeth so heavily jewelled there seemed more diamond there than calcite.

There was nothing to do but shield my eyes and mouth, presenting my curled back to them as they drove their boots into my ribs and spine and the back of my skull, over and over, blurring the world into darkness and blood. Finally, once they'd exhausted their enthusiasm for violence, Diedrick gripped me by the hair and held my head back while each of them went about the ordered business of spitting into my face. The waif took the first turn, turning up a truly admirable quantity of spittle. It splattered, stinking and gelatinous, against my lacerated cheek and stayed there like a clot of glue while the others stepped up to add their own bile to the stew.

I was bedridden for several weeks after the assault. But I did not despair in my infirmity, for though it had ended badly, my time spent among the cultists had not been without value. For via their concourse I had made contact with those apostates among the dental profession to whom they offered their patronage. It was in that society of blackguard prosthodontists that I first heard whispers of that man who would become my closest ally. An innovator in his field who was nonetheless exiled from his chosen profession for reasons of moral turpitude and what were called gross abuses of dental science. When first I heard the name of the American Dr. Alphonse Meridian I knew that we were kindred souls, incensed by the same passion, bound in desolation by the same strange pursuit. His was a mind that would mirror my own. The more I dwelled on him, as I lay helpless and abandoned to my slow convalescence in that Berlin hotel room, the more certain I became that Dr. Meridian had been brought to me by fate.

The attack by the philistine tooth-fanatics had left me with a fracture in my hip bone which was agonizingly slow to heal. Waried by recent experiences, I purchased an ivory handled walking stick in which was concealed 18 inches of steel sharp enough to sever an artery. On the suggestion of a German physician with whom I was able to communicate only through translation by a somewhat harried nurse, I increased my intake of chlorodyne to alleviate the pain of my injured body and pride, and booked passage to England, where the American dentist was rumoured to have fled.

It was on the train through Belgium that I had the most lucid vision I had experienced since my time in the asylum. It was during a thunderstorm which raged all across the fields of Brussels, cascading hail upon the steel roof of the sleeping car and piercing the lurid night with flashes of lightning and winds sharp and strong enough to test the integrity of many a peasant cottage we passed along the track. Though leadened by my most recent dose of chlorodyne, I pushed myself up atop the birth in my private compartment so that I might part the curtains and watch the tempest unfold.

The night greeted me with a flash of lightning so bright and close it may have been hurled at me directly by Jupiter himself, yet I did not start or fall back. Through the translucent glass, amid the drapery of fog that fell across the wheat fields, I saw Her speak to me in that secret language of mystery and calamity. The night winds bore aloft the golden cascade of her hair, the lightning flashed with all the colours of her insectile wings, the grey mist formed the contours of her face.

And then I slept, despite what had been raging above my head. Strangely, when I spoke to my fellow English-speaking passengers about the storm, I was met with bafflement and misunderstanding, as if the night had passed in peaceful somnolence and I was but a madman, mistaking his own nightmares for nature's true rage.

Three weeks later I arrived in London and checked myself into the Empress of India Hotel in Mayfair, which kept its best room reserved in perpetua for the Queen, despite her never having expressed any interest in staying there. Regardless, my suite was adequately comfortable, and I resumed my life's work with utmost haste.

Through contacts I had made during my time in Berlin, I was able to procure a fairly recent address for the good dentist, who it seemed had adopted a fairly nomadic lifestyle since his exile from the profession. The room was in a dilapidated boarding house on the edge of a neighbourhood that can only be described as gangrenous, hanging off of London like a decaying limb. Buildings were in gross disrepair; unwashed, drunken barbarians stumbled through the streets with idiotic grimaces and empty eyes.

I questioned his former landlady, lining her gnarled palm with silver to loosen her tongue. In a garbled butchery of that language which her own native country had fathered, she related to me the good doctor's habits. It seemed he had developed a taste for intoxicating substances lately utilized in dental surgery, some common to the profession, others preparations of his own devising. His predilection for exotic pharmaceuticals, however, was not the reason the old crone gave for having demanded an end to his residency in her six room hovel. It seemed the good doctor had been performing scientific inquiries of an esoteric nature, luring vagabonds back to the boarding house with promises of food or refreshment, and subjecting them to experiments which often left them legless as if with drink, comatose, or raving. Though few residents of that neighbourhood could have boasted a full set of healthy teeth to begin with (the landlady added this fact without prompt, while displaying her own rot-blackened molars) all of Alphonse Meridian's guests, without exception, left the good doctor's room with none at all. Though she had long ago become accustomed to all manner of excessive oddness, the hag said with finality, the other boarders had been bothered by the screams.

My patience soon became short with the old woman's prattle, and I was soon pervaded upon to offer further largess in exchange for a succinct description of where Dr. Meridian could currently be found. Ill-gotten bounty in hand, the old crone

thanked me profusely, and I continued on my way

with sound, if circuitous, directions.

The address and circumstances in which I

found Dr. Meridian were reduced at best, and at

worst, outright deplorable. Since taking his leave of

the boarding house, the good doctor had taken up

residence in the cheapest and most squalid sort of

brothel, where he provided dental care for those

among the foul and aging assortment of fallen

women inhabiting the house who still possessed

teeth, and created passably life-like facsimiles

there-of for those who did not.

You may ask if it angered me to see a genius

of Dr. Alphonse Meridian's calibre and a colleague

in my own life's work reduced to such employment

by the disavowal of that society of apes and luddites

who make up the modern dental profession. And yes, I was angered. But not so much that I did not recognise the opportunity that the doctor's reduction afforded me.

I walked up the three broken steps to the crimson-painted door of the bawdy house, its entryway flanked by ornate iron sculptures moulting bronze leaf, and knocked. The door was promptly answered by an overflowing mess of female flesh stuffed into a corset and bloomers that had all been stained a vile, uneven pink. Her mouth opened in a lopsided smile, showing off a mouthful of clay dentures painted the unlikely, bluish-white shade of a French tea service.

I asked for Dr. Meridian, and the disappointed wench led me down into the basement room where the doctor resided. She opened the door without knocking, revealing the sight of a skeletal, sickly man in paint splattered shirtsleeves and bracers, squinting through a glass magnifier at the set of false teeth he was painting with glossy enamel. His face was unshaven, obscuring the presence of what may have once been a dignified moustache, and his lank hair had gone untrimmed for a long, long time. As the whore left without introducing me and I was hesitant to interrupt his thoroughly absorbing work, I merely stood and watched the good dentist, unbeknownst to him, for some time. Shortly he stopped to regard his work and, seemingly satisfied with it, placed his paintbrush in a mason jar of solvent and rewarded himself with a lungful of gas sucked via rubber hose from a brass cylinder next to his pressboard-and-masonry-brick workbench. It was mid-inhalation that I announced myself, startling the doctor and causing him to gasp and choke on the illicit vapour.

"Who the devil are you?" he asked, his voice rendered faint and squeaky by whatever toxins he was imbibing.

"I'm your newest patron," I told him, for I doubted he would make any argument against it. "I'm offering you a chance to leave this slum and continue your research."

"What research?" The doctor growled, his long, paint-stained hand rising to wipe a bead of drool from his cracked lips.

"I know who you are, doctor," I told him plainly, "I know about the experiments you were conducting, why you were asked to leave the University of North Carolina and came here to

London. And more importantly, I know about the secret obsession that drives you."

The doctor furrowed his brow, then looked away. "You can't possibly know that," he said.

"But I do, doctor, for it is the same obsession that drives me."

The dentist turned, and looked me in the eye. "Then God save us both."

"I don't answer to any God," I said, "Only to the Tooth Fairy."

"You're mad," Dr. Meridian said, eyeing his brass canister, "We're all mad. The Tooth Fairy is a myth, a story for children."

"She isn't," I said, "I've seen her."

This declaration seemed to inspire some consternation in the doctor for he rose from his seat and began to pace the small room, circling the clutter that included a large dentist's chair made of rusted steel and equipped with leather restraints that were worn and stained, but looked to be sturdy.

"Of course you've seen her," Dr. Meridian said, "I've seen her. Any child that's teethed and gained possession of a pillow has seen her and been rewarded with one of her godforsaken tokens. But no one has seen her since, have they?"

"No," I replied, my heart swelling with melancholy at the thought. I have had glimpses, perhaps tricks of fever or the light, and more dreams of her than I could count. But had I truly seen her as I had when I was a child? That answer was simple, I had not.

Dr. Meridian grinned savagely, taking pleasure in my sorrow. "And I bet you've tried, haven't you? I bet you've done everything you could think of, placed teeth beneath your pillow by the handful, and nothing. Am I right?"

Loath as I was to admit it, he was right. I nodded silently.

"What does that make us, then?" The doctor asked. When I didn't answer, he answered for me. "A couple of obsessives. A couple of madmen who should be living decently, raising families, wasting our goddamned lives chasing shadows. Fantasy stories are for children. Adults know there's no such thing as goddesses or fairy princesses. There's no such thing as the Tooth Fairy."

My mouth gaped in wordless horror. I could not believe what I was hearing. I had travelled the world seeking a kindred spirit who would aid me in my quest for that which was perfect and unnameable. For all I had heard about his research, could the good dentist be nothing more than another complacent fool? How could I have been so wrong?

Then Dr. Meridian's eyes closed and an expression came onto his face that can only be described as one of pure, perfect rapture, "What she is," he said, "Is so much more than that."

Part IV:

The Realm of the Ancients

The whores had complained that the good doctor's experiments had been negatively impacting their business, the seeking of transcendence running afoul of base desire. So Dr. Meridian was forced to perform his experiments between the unlikely hours of four and eight am, when custom was at its most infrequent. Being somewhat of a night creature myself, I did not object. I could, in fact, think of no more appropriate time for our work than that still and haunted hour. In the setting as well, the peeling walls, the stench, and the choir of grunts prevailing upon us from the floors above, there seemed a sort of horrid poetry.

Dr. Meridian did not look at me as he steadfastly began to unbox and sort the collection of flasks and leather wrapped vials of chemicals my patronage had allowed him to purchase, uncorking some and sniffing them gingerly, holding others up to the lights to study their clarity or liquidity.

"The key," the doctor told me, "Is to recreate the mind of the child, that precious innocence she sniffs out like a shark after blood."

We were never innocent, but still, I take his meaning.

"You will lie down," he said, still not looking at me as he uncorked a vial and began to mix chemicals upon his paint-stained platform.

With some reluctance, I propped my sword-cane against a wall and lay down upon the layer of thin, filthy padding that had been glued down to the iron seat of the rusted dentist's chair. As I settled myself, I was seized by an unexpected dread as recollections of my time in the asylum flooded my mind with a lucidity which startled me.

I gasped aloud, my teeth clenching, and swung my fist in violent defence against nothing but a draft of air.

The doctor appeared not to notice my apprehension, absorbed as he was in the mixing of chemicals.

"You see nothing spiritual in our work at all, then?" I asked the good doctor. Perhaps it was the wrong time for such a question, but there would be no other time.

"Spiritualism," Dr. Meridian answered, "Is a word for fields of science which man, so far, lacks the ability to comprehend. Likewise, evil is a word for those fields of scientific inquiry which man does not wish to comprehend. However, if it pleases you to call her a goddess, I will not object."

"Not when I'm offering you funding, you mean," I said to him, "Pray there be no illusions between us."

He looked up very briefly, before hunching back over those potions and fetishes of his trade. "As I say, you may believe what you choose to believe."

Sudden curiosity fused with that strange melancholy which had so burdened me of late, and I could not help but ask, "What do you call her, then? When the night is dark and lonely, the obsession rages in you like a fever, and there is no way open to you but that path which leads to Hell or revelation?"

Dr. Meridian looked up from his work and stared thoughtfully into the single candle which augmented the meagre flickering of the electric lights. His eyes, for a moment, seemed both blank and eagle-like in the breadth of their perception. "I don't know," he said in a slow, quiet voice, "She is the divine other, I suppose. Speaking objectively, I believe she is a trans-dimensional being so far beyond us in scientific and evolutionary advancement that we are able to perceive her in nothing but the most abstract terms, as a fairy, or a phantom."

"And subjectively?" I ask, lowering myself down onto the stinking foam mat. My hands gripped the ridged edges on either side of the chair and I felt the straps there, hard cold leather dangling from steel chains bolted tightly to the arm rests.

He tilted his head slightly, a strangely placid, thoughtful expression seeming out-of-place on his wild, unshaven countenance. "Subjectively," he said,

"In that dark and lonely night of which you speak, I suppose I call her demon, for the possibility of absolution it might afford me to have been led astray by some infernal thing, and not the other way."

"So we are hellbound, then?" I asked him. It wasn't the first time I'd asked the question, even aloud, even to a near stranger. It was not to be the last.

"Would it stop you if we were?"

I did not give him an answer, for I knew none was needed.

The doctor stood and approached my side with a peculiar timidity that I found fascinating. He fastened the leather straps around my wrists and ankles amidst apologies for their necessity, subjects tended to thrash and buck, exposing themselves to injury. Lastly he opened my mouth, and probed my teeth with a gloved hand that tasted of soap and rubber. I tensed at this, recalling old horrors, but his touch was as different from that late mutilation as it possibly could have been. His touch was tentative, gentle, but very thorough.

Lastly, he retrieved a canister he had filled with some nebulous substance, appearing through the translucent glass like a slab of ice slowly vulcanizing into a gas. He attached the tube connecting it to the anaesthesia mask, an unpleasant rubber cup that fit snugly over my nose and mouth, and turned a valve.

Breathing in mouthfuls of perfumed air, I thought of my sister for the first time in years. Is this how her death had felt? This slow saturation of sweet toxicity? As my body fought instinctively for oxygen, my breaths came in deeper and more frequent gasps and I did not resist, knowing as I did that each breath served to hasten my descent, propelling me further towards the Tooth Fairy. I breathed in eagerly, though my lungs ached and my brain seemed ready to burst inside my skull. To distract myself from the agony I studied the substance in the doctor's canister, the riot of colours that were produced as the chemicals reacted: gold, crimson, indigo and emerald. Something glistened deep within: a pale silver moon in orbit around a blue giant, a supernova, and in the apex of this microcosmic universe, a black hole devouring all light, all thought, all sentience and purpose, bringing everything back to a bleak and broken darkness.

She came to me then, out of the blackness

that bordered death. She drifted before me in

caliginosity of night, an oasis in the purgatorial

nothing and nowhere into which I had been

propelled. In all her glory, she was as I had recalled

her in the shadowed witch-land of my deepest

fantasies. The arching rainbow of her wings formed

a crescent around her, like an angel's halo, except for

those topmost two which, as always, veiled her

perfect mouth. She looked at me, her spiralling eyes

peering curiously beneath the crowned, golden arch

of her brow, and I knew she perceived me, then, in

mind and soul. She saw me and she spoke to me,

not in words, but like a river rushing, like birdcalls

and thunder and the mysteries of all nature. Her

pale arm, clothed in glimmering samite, reached out

to me across the abyss.

No longer bound, I put out my hand and she grasped it. At her touch, I wept.

The good doctor had done as he had promised! The Tooth Fairy had come for me at last! My Goddess! The marvel of my heart! I flew with her across the emerald forests and snow-capped mountains where dwelled creatures of myth and magic. I flew above those crystalline cities, veined with streets of gleaming gold whereupon walked ancient creatures of genius and beauty, long forgotten by mankind.

I wept with joy, and as I wept my tears crystallized into radiant, multifaceted diamonds which floated and hung before me in the blue velvet sky. And miraculously, before my eyes, the diamonds embedded themselves in the fabric of that indigo night and became as stars.

I can't say for how long our journey lasted, for I felt as if I had transcended time. Somewhere far away my flesh may have been dying, suffocating, but my mind soared. Finally, after a period of drifting that may have lasted for hours or centuries, we came near the apex of a great mountain range. Jagged turrets of black crystal, veined with white and rose quartz, piercing a sky that had attained a colour and luminance like the blue-hot heart of a flame, but from which a cold wind whispered down. And in this crystal mountain was a cave, massive and yawning, its oval mouth ringed with smooth white stalactites. Bidden by my fairy guide, my feet finally touched down on the cavern floor. Its floor was not hard obsidian, like the exterior of the mountain, but porous and red, infused with heat as if from some hidden hot-spring. I heard the rushing of water echoing amongst the cavern walls, and felt a warm, salted breeze. Were we near the sea? That miraculous, endless blue sea I remembered from my childhood reverie: where mermaids frolicked beneath those peaked and frosted waves?

I clasped the Fairy's hand, that smooth silken hand, and felt that I would never let it go, even should it lead me into the very mouth of madness itself.

She brought me deeper into the cave, to where the rock floor ended at a cliff's edge overlooking a deeper and broader expanse of cavern. This cavern, perhaps hundreds of metres deep and wide thought I did not trust, in that place of aberrance, my perception of space anymore than my perception of time, was filled to brimming with a multitude of figures, clothed in ragged robes, bowing as if in abjection. They clustered together, filling the space to bursting, sustaining only the vaguest shapes of men. With my dream-eyes I could see it all with perfect clarity, my vision untempered by distance or dimness. It was not necessary for me to focus my eyes on any particular aspect of the tableau, for I found I could view all figures and objects within my field of vision at once and individually, in equal detail. This, perhaps, was the greatest horror.

A cacophony of chatter, pierced now and again by an agonizing screech, filled the cavern. The creatures beneath me rose up onto their haunches, arched their backs and spread their insectile wings. Their bodies were squat, their faces split in the center by a massive gash of a mouth which housed fangs so large and unwieldy that they pierced through that fold of flesh which resided where a human's lip might be, mangling it. Black blood dripped from their lacerated faces, down between their thin, elongated legs and falling in heavy droplets from the tips of those narrow, antennae-like appendages that may have been their genitalia. Their heads were like the heads of sharks — huge and bulbous with protruding jaws. Their skin was grey and had the appearance of stone. It was only by their bugging, multi-coloured eyes and their wings, like enlarged, colourless shadows of those wings I knew so well, which revealed the truth of their existence to me. I had never wondered if there were others of her kind; it had never occurred to me to do so. The Tooth Fairy was an absolute:

eternal and inscrutable. I had never considered her genealogy. How stupid I had been! How atrociously idiotic! It had never entered my mind that there may be a male of her species.

There were others like her: beautiful, ethereal creatures wandering amongst the grotesques. Many females carried casks and sacks of broken and bloody teeth. They spilled them out in yellowing heaps upon the red stone floor, gesturing at them and chattering in their strange, twittering tongue. The grotesques looked up at them dumbly, their red tongues lolling out of their horrid, barbarized faces. Their shovel-shaped fingers scooped up the piles of teeth from the floor and delivered them into their mouths greedily, with abandon. They sucked them down whole, cackling, slurping, swallowing.

The females were obviously dominant:
issuing commands, dispensing rewards, and herding
their brothers and mates about the cavern.
However, there were so few of them! I counted only
six, while the males were uncountable, a veritable
legion.

And at the far front of the swarm, spread
lank and bloated upon a stone podium, lay the
queen.

She was larger and broader than the other
females, even discounting the grossly bloated belly,
big enough to be containing within it an entity at
least as large as a human youth. She seemed
immobile beneath the weight of it, pinned down
upon her rocky bed like a butterfly to a child's bit of
corkboard. Her wings appeared almost comically
small in contrast, warped and useless beneath her

massive bulk. She wheezed and shrieked, naked even of the diaphanous robes worn by the other females. Her over-stretched skin was translucent, revealing beneath the shape and texture, the bright, sickly colour and sheer abundance of the eggs that filled her bare and quivering gut, almost to the point of bursting.

Flanking her on all sides were the grotesques, bowing and scraping, scratching at the dirt with their flat shovel-like fingers, hundreds of them, thousands. They were scraping at the cave walls, at the gleaming obsidian that filled the spaces between the great expanse of crumbling red floor, digging around the roots of the great white stalactites, the size of marble pillars in some cathedral of terror. I turned away in horror, unable to accept the vision before me. All around me these creatures: digging, mining, breeding, doing their wicked work to free from its stone entombment that massive beast in whose open mouth they all resided.

I don't recall at what precise moment I began to scream.

***

I woke with a scoured throat, soaked in sweat and still strapped down to the filthy dentist's chair in that whorehouse basement. My hands pulled at the straps at my side but they held fast.

I screamed, though my voice was broken. I cursed and called out for Dr. Meridian, but there came no answer to my call. The good doctor sat slumped ignobly upon his workbench, quite dead.

In the end, it was the whores who responded to my screams. They unfastened the straps and hurried me out of the house, already descending upon the poor, dead doctor. In the weeks that followed his death would be pronounced due to misadventure, an ether overdose, but I knew the truth. I'd gone to him before I was ushered out, pried open his stiffened jaw and found what I both knew and feared I would find: all of his teeth had been removed bloodily, his gums savaged. He had been the only friend I'd ever had, save Augusta, yet I had no pity to spare him. I left London the next day, and not a word was heard about Doctor Meridian again.

Which brings us to the present, and to this, my final testament: I have travelled beyond the realms of men and found no solace there, nor peace, nor salvation. Only terror lies beyond this realm of blood and tears, and it is a terror which has struck to the very heart of me. I have been rendered mad, doomed, and hellhound beyond reckoning, for I have pledged myself to that dire Mistress of Hell, that infernal thief of man's most immortal parts: the Tooth Fairy.

Even now I can feel her presence, the slender, invisible hands pressing into my jaw, pulling, wrenching. Are they the hands of madness, or of the Fairy? No matter, soon it shall all be over.

I have purchased my salvation in the form of an ultra-modern electric device recently patented by a young American inventor. The device consists of a mobile sanding belt driven by an electric motor. I'm told it's used by common labourers to smooth surfaces when constructing furniture. With this instrument in hand I have returned to Ivory Oak manor for the first time in more years than I can anymore recall.

When she comes for me, there must be nothing left for her to claim. The rest of my mortal flesh I shall submit to immolation. But teeth will not burn.

If the new electric motor shall fail me, I may resort to some other implement. There will be tools in the caretaker's shed. The pain is nothing to me, for I know what lies beyond the veil. I have seen the awful truth of the Tooth Fairy and all her malformed and malignant kin, and there is no end for me but the asylum or the fire.

I press the rough sanding surface against the bottom row of my teeth. My trembling fingers fumble to engage the motor.

That pain...that exquisite pain. My mouth fills with blood and the scrapped flesh of my tongue, and for a moment I glimpse her once again in all her majesty. Through the blinding pain, I see the wings fold down from her face and I glimpse her naked mouth.

It is...transcendent.

ABOUT THE AUTHOR

Sebastian Gray is a Vancouver based writer of dark fantasy and horror fiction. Her stories have been featured in Subterrain, Planet Scumm, and on the NoSleep podcast. She is generally a much sweeter and more optimistic person than her fiction would indicate, although she does sometimes wonder if we weren't all swallowed by a carnivorous space god sometime in the nineties, and if 'reality' as we know it isn't the product of hallucinogens excreted by its unfathomably slow digestive system. Sebastian lives in a tower by a train station with her childhood best friend and a collection of stuffed animals.